THIS IS GEORGE BEARD AND HAROLD HUTCHINS.

GEORGE is the kid with the tie and flat-top. **HAROLD** is the one with the bad haircut. Remember that now. Except tonight, George is actually Harold and Harold is actually George, because they're dressed as each other for Halloween.

GEORGE

HAROLD

Every year, George and Harold go trick-or-treating together. Every. Single. Year. Because they love Halloween! It's the one night that using toilet paper to turn your neighbors' trees into mummies and going door-to-door in strange outfits begging for treats is socially acceptable. Except for that one year that turned everything upside down.

THE HORRIFYINGLY HAUNTED YEAR OF HACK-A-WEEN . . .

I **LOVE** Hallowarehouse. It's all the best parts of Halloween. Fake skulls. Fake eyeballs. Fake vampire fangs. REAL flashlights. All crammed under one roof!

Camping outside so we're first in line is the greatest idea we've ever had. Almost as good as the trick we played on Melvin last year.

MELLLVINNN...

ZOMBIE PLUMBERS?! BUT I DON'T WANT TO BE EATEN **OR** HAVE MY SINK FIXED!

It's a good thing Melvin loves Halloween as much as we do. Otherwise, that prank could have had some really unexpected consequences.

I can't believe that actually happened. Halloween is canceled!
We need to make the adults remember what's great about Halloween. And there's only one adult who loves Halloween as much as we do.
You don't mean . . .
Old Man Rattlechains. The owner of Hallowarehouse!

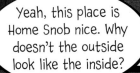

This is going perfectly.

Just a few more festively frightening scares, and all the parents will be sure to sign our petition to un-cancel Halloween!

That's what you think! I've turned your fake haunted house into a REAL nightmare with my Inanimanitator 2000. It brings lifeless objects to life!

And now, when your living Halloween decorations scare the adults to death, it will be the death of Halloween . . . FOREVER!

MWA-HA-HA-HA-HA!

CHAPTER 4
THE INCREDIBLY SCARY BATTLE CHAPTER
STARRING CAPTAIN UNDERPANTS

EYYYYYYEEEEEEEEEEE!!!!

So one time, there was this bad guy named Holihater who hated holidays, especially Halloween.

And he used a Holiray to vaporize all the town's Halloween stuff.

ANYONE WHO SAYS HALLOWEEN GETS VAPORIZED, TOO!

That put a crimp in Captain Underpants's Monster Mash plans. But the Waistband Warrior came up with a Hall-o-riffic work-around. He hacked his Halloween party into an ALL-o-ween party! Instead of spooky decorations, everyone brought whatever they felt like. Pillows. Drywall. Tires.

And instead of costumes, they dressed up in disguises like Doctorca, an orca who went to med school. And Frobra, a frozen cobra.

And since their party wasn't Halloween but ALL-O-WEEN, they could totally get down without fear of being vaporized!

So, Captain Underpants welcomed him. And Holihater promised not to vaporize holidays anymore. Everyone had a blast, until the police showed up because of noise complaints. TOO LOUD!

The ENd!

CHAPTER 6
TWEEN WEEN FIGHTING MACHINE

George and Harold explained their plan to the rest of the kids at Jerome Horwitz Elementary

(except for Melvin, obviously).

Do you really think Hack-A-Ween will work?

Yes! Instead of costumes, we'll wear disguises. Instead of trick-or-treating, we'll go sneak-or-snacking. There's nothing illegal about that!

MEANWHILE . . .

George and Harold have posted an online video guide to . . . **Hack-A-Ween**?

Hack-A-Ween oReeuNtAshun

● REC

ARGH! I shouldn't be surprised those demagnetized magnets found a loophole in Hall-NO-ween. Time to come up with a plan B. . .

Outside Hallowarehouse . . .

Wait. Melvin didn't go trick-or-treating with us last year. Or the year before. Come to think of it, I don't think he's EVER gone with us.

THAT'S why Melvin hates Halloween. He's never been invited to join in, just like Holihater in our comic!
Then there's only one thing to do.

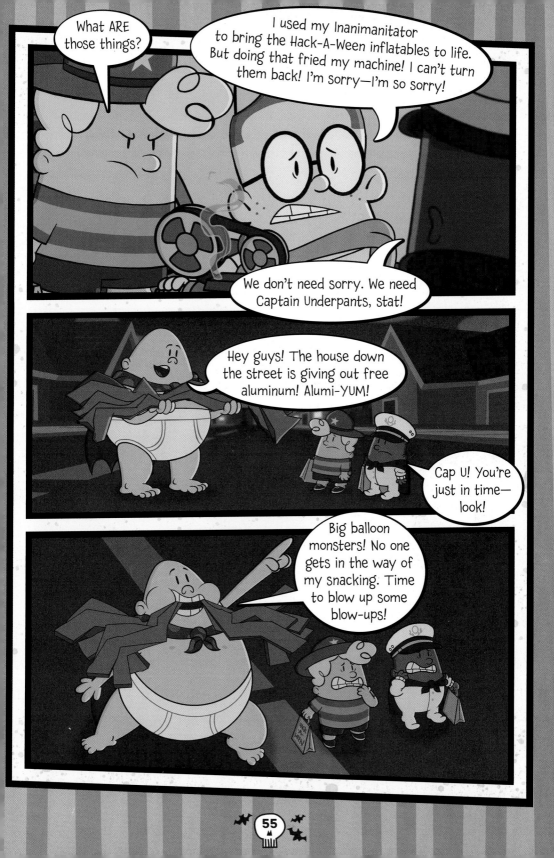